The Dog Who Cried Wolf

KEIKO KASZA

SCHOLASTIC INC.

New York Toronto London Auckland Sydney
Mexico City New Delhi Hong Kong Buenos Aires

This book is dedicated to Kyoka.

And a special thanks to the real Moka,
Moka Latham-Brown, the pet dog of my friends.
His lively personality was the inspiration for the book.

ISBN-13: 978-0-439-89568-2
ISBN-10: 0-439-89568-5

12 11 10 9 8 7 6 5 4 3 2 1   6 7 8 9 10 11/0

Printed in the U.S.A.   40

First Scholastic printing, October 2006

Design by Gunta Alexander.
Text set in Angie.

Moka was a good dog. He and Michelle loved to be together. Life was perfect, until one day, she read a book about wolves.

"Look, Moka," said Michelle, "you're kind of like a wolf!"

Wow! thought Moka. I *am* kind of like a wolf. But look how amazing wolves are! They run around free, hunt wild animals, and stay up late to howl at the moon.

And look at the way I live, Moka sighed. I'm nothing but a house pet. He felt like a failure, especially when Michelle made him dress up for her tea parties. He wanted to be a wolf.

The next day, Moka made up his mind. He snuck out of the house and took off for the mountains. He ran, and ran, and ran . . .

. . . until finally he reached a high mountaintop.
"I'm free!" he yelped. "Free as a wolf!"

He ran.

He jumped.

He danced.

And he peed wherever
he wanted.
"Wow!" he exclaimed.
"The world is mine!"

Soon, Moka got hungry. "No problem!" he cried.
"I'll hunt for my food, just like the wolves do."
And off he went.

But a rabbit outran him.

A skunk sprayed him.

A beetle pinched him.

And even a field mouse
made fun of him.

By nightfall, Moka was miserable. He missed Michelle.
"I even miss her tea parties," he mumbled. "But I can't
give up yet. There is just one more thing I have to try . . ."

He gazed at the golden moon and howled as loudly as he could: "Haooooooooo . . . ," just like a wolf.

Suddenly, something howled back! "Haooooooo . . .
Haoooooo . . ." and then again, "Haoooooo . . ."
Moka froze.
"Wooooooooolves!" he cried. "Real wolves!"

He turned and raced down the mountain. "I want to go home!" he panted. "I never want to be a wolf again!"

He ran, and ran, and ran . . .

MAIL

Missing Dog!
Answers to Moka
Call Michelle
at

. . . until finally he reached the house he knew so
well.

"Moka!" Michelle shouted as she dashed out to
meet him.

"You're back!"

Moka was home again, and he and Michelle were oh, so happy! Life was just perfect, until one day, she read a book about monkeys. . . .